BRIGHT and EARLY BOOKS
for BEGINNING Beginners

BOOK CLUB EDITION

HE BEAR SHE BEAR

by Stan and Jan Berenstain

A Bright & Early Book

From BEGINNER BOOKS
A Division of Random House, Inc., New York

For Leo and Robin

 Published in the United States by Random House, Inc., New York, and simultaneously in Canada by Random House of Canada Limited, Toronto. Library of Congress Cataloging in Publication Data: Berenstain, Stanley. He bear, she bear. (A Bright & early book, 20) SUMMARY: Two little bears, a brother and sister, speculate on all the things they could grow up to be. [1. Occupations—Fiction. 2. Stories in rhyme] I. Berenstain, Janice, joint author. II. Title. PZ8.3.B4493He [E] 74-5518 ISBN 0-394-82997-2 ISBN 0-394-92997-7 (lib. bdg.) Manufactured in the United States of America.

P Q R 890

HE BEAR
SHE BEAR

I see her.
She sees me.

We see that we
are he and she.

Every single
bear we see
is a he bear
or a she.

Every single
bear we see
has lots of things
to do and be.

I'm a father.
I'm a he.
A father's something
you could be.

I'm a mother.
I'm a she.
A mother's something
you could be.

Dad's a he.
Mom's a she.

Those are things
that we could be
just because
we're he and she.

But there are
other things to be.
Come on, He Bear,
follow me!

We could . . .

fix a clock,

paint a door,

build a house,

have a store.

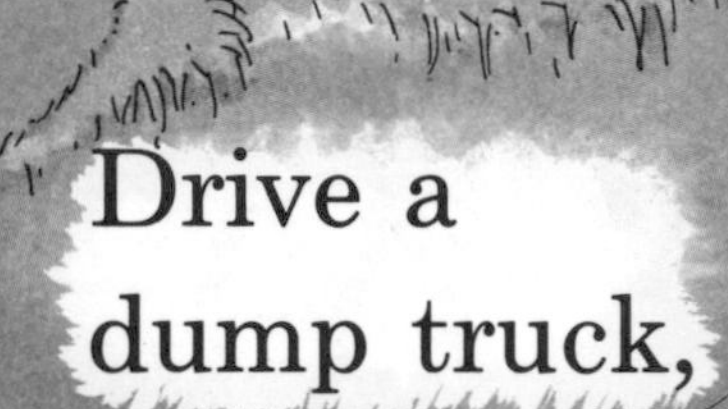

Drive a
dump truck,

drive a crane,

bulldoze roads,

drive a train.

We fix clocks,
we paint doors,
we build houses,
we have stores.

We bulldoze roads,
we drive cranes,
we drive trucks,
we drive trains.

We can do all these things,
you see,
whether we are he or she.

We climb ladders
to fix the wires.

We climb ladders
to put out fires.

That's Officer Marguerite.
She tells us when
to cross the street.

You could . . .

Be a doctor—
make folks well.

Teach kids how
to add and spell.

Knit a sock,

sew a dress,

paint a picture—

what a mess!

You could . . .

Lead a band,
sing a song,
play a tuba,
beat a gong.

Play a banjo—
plink-a-plink.
You could even play
on a kitchen sink.

We have stores,
we fix clocks,
we are officers,
we knit socks.

We teach kids how
to add and spell,
we drive, we build,
we make folks well.

We climb ladders,
we sew dresses,
we make music,
we make messes.

We can do all these things,
you see,
whether we are he or she.

What will <u>we</u> do,
you and I?

I'll tell you what
I'm going to try . . .

I may build bridges,

I may climb poles,

I may race cars,

I may dig holes.

I could be a magician,

I could go on TV,

I could study the fish
who live in the sea.

I'll be a cowboy,

I'll go to the moon,

I'll feed a whale,

I'll train a baboon.

We'll fly a giant
jumbo jet.

We'll build the tallest building yet.

We will jump
on a trampoline.

We'll do tricks
that have never
been seen.

We'll tame
twelve tigers . . .

and twenty-six fleas.

We'll do a dance
on a flying trapeze.

We'll jump and dig
and build and fly. . . .
There's <u>nothing</u> that
we cannot try.

We can do all these things,
you see,
whether we are he OR she.

So <u>many</u> <u>things</u>
to be and do,
He Bear, She Bear,
me . . . and you.

Stan and Jan Berenstain

For years Stan and Jan Berenstain were well-known to millions of adult readers for their many marvelously funny books and magazine features on family life in America. Then, with THE BIG HONEY HUNT, children discovered that they also wrote marvelously funny books about family life in Bear Country. Since then millions of beginning readers have enjoyed the misadventures of the famous Bear Family.

The Berenstains went to the same art school (the Philadelphia Museum School), enjoy the same food, tastes and hobbies, have the same two sons, and as far as can be discovered, type simultaneously on the same typewriter and draw simultaneously on the same piece of paper. They work together in the same studio in Elkins Park, Pennsylvania, creating words and pictures that delight bears and children around the world.